To my children Sophia, Amber and Oliver.

To all families approaching the end of their breast/chestfeeding journey; I hope this book brings comfort, relief and validation. Celebrate this milestone and be proud of what you have achieved!

Goodbye Mummy's Milk!

ISBN: 978-1-7396299-0-8

Illustration and design by happydesigner.
www.happydesigner.co.uk

Goodbye Mummy's Milk!

Mariapaola Weeks

Illustrated by Sarah-Leigh Wills

About the Author

Mariapaola Weeks BSc, PGDip (Specialist Community Public Health Nursing, King's College London) is a health visitor and children's nurse, living and working in London. With over 10 years' experience working as a paediatric nurse, Mariapaola has a special interest in supporting families with infant feeding and relationship building. Mariapaola, a mother of three, was inspired to write *Goodbye Mummy's Milk!* when preparing her eldest children for the end of their breastfeeding journey, whilst experiencing nursing aversion.

Support and Information

Support and information with weaning and/or with nursing aversion can be found at: the Association of Breastfeeding Mothers (https://abm.me.uk), the Breastfeeding Network (https://www.breastfeedingnetwork.org.uk) and La Leche League GB (https://www.laleche.org.uk).

You can find a qualified lactation consultant, local to you, at Lactation Consultants of Great Britain (https://lcgb.org/find-an-ibclc/). Emma Pickett IBCLC (https://www.emmapickettbreastfeedingsupport.com) specialises in supporting with older children and stopping breastfeeding.

There are also free support groups on Facebook, including Aversion Sucks! Breastfeeding Aversion Peer-to-peer Support and Breastfeeding Older Babies and Beyond. For anyone who is feeling negative emotions associated with ending breastfeeding before they are ready, I recommend 'Why Breastfeeding Grief and Trauma Matter' by Amy Brown.

As I clamber into bed
And snuggle under my quilt,
My Mummy suddenly says...
"Soon it will be time to say goodbye to Mummy's milk!"

This makes me feel confused;
I want to shout and scream.
"Does Mummy not know that
It's better than ice cream?"

My Mummy's milk is everything,
Everything and more.
My Mummy's milk is certainly
All I could wish for.

My Mummy's milk is magical,
It is unique, nutritious.
My Mummy's milk is healing,
It is super delicious.

My Mummy's milk is calming,
Comforting and safe.
My Mummy's milk is always there,
In my own warm, special place.

But something strange is happening,
Something very mad.
My Mummy's milk is going away,
And making us all sad.

Mummy says, "It hurts!"
It sometimes makes her cry.
I say, "Mummy, I'll be gentle.
Please, just one more try?"

Mummy pleads, "Stop twiddling!
Try the other side!"
Even though I try my best,
My Mummy wants to hide.

Mummy growls "I'm tired.
I can't breastfeed like this forever."
But I am tired too,
And I need her more than ever.

I ask my Mummy once again,
"Please, just a little sip?"
I tell her: "I will open wide.
I'll be really quick!"

But my Mummy turns to me
Her voice is like a ROAR:
"It hurts so much, I've had enough,
I can't do this anymore!"

This makes me so upset.
These feelings I can't bear.
I want to run, this isn't fun,
This seems like a nightmare.

Mummy soothes me with a hug:
"It's natural to feel sad
Till we get weaning wings and learn
Growing up can make us glad!"

"Whenever you're missing Mummy's milk
or feeling rather blue,
We can cuddle together, bath together,
There's lots that we can do."

"We can read together, draw together,
Play with trains and cars.
Bounce a ball, sing a song,
Paint shiny silver stars."

Mummy explains just how her milk
Has achieved fantastic things.
It is so very powerful.
With everything it brings.

I can splash and paddle in streams,
And I can run so fast.
I feel like I have superpowers,
That will always last.

Mummy's milk has built an invisible armour,
A shield against those who are sick,
And an immunity-boosting army,
Which helps me to get better so quick.

And now I can eat lots of foods
Like vegetables, fruits and seeds.

To keep me strong and healthy,
These are mostly what I need.

Mummy's milk has helped me know
When I'm hungry and when I'm full,
Which is the perfect way to grow,
From small to really tall!

It's taught me all about feelings,
And relationships and friends.
It has shown me how to be kind and gentle
And that our love will never end.

My Mummy's milk has given me
The confidence to explore.
I can climb over mountains,
And play in rock pools by the shore.

When I venture a little too far,
Or feel frightened or alone,
I will have my weaning wings,
Which I'll soon have fully grown.

All that I will need to do,
Is imagine them open wide.
Call out for my Mummy,
And fly back to her side.

Being close to you, Mummy,
Makes me realise you are the best.
You have shared all your strength.
Now I can safely leave your breast!

Before I say "Goodbye Mummy's milk!"
I really want you to know
How proud I am of every drop
That you've given me to thrive and grow.

So "Thank you, my dear Mummy,
For everything you've done and do.
The person I am today
Is greatly because of you."

Now that the time is here,
I'm feeling bold and brave.

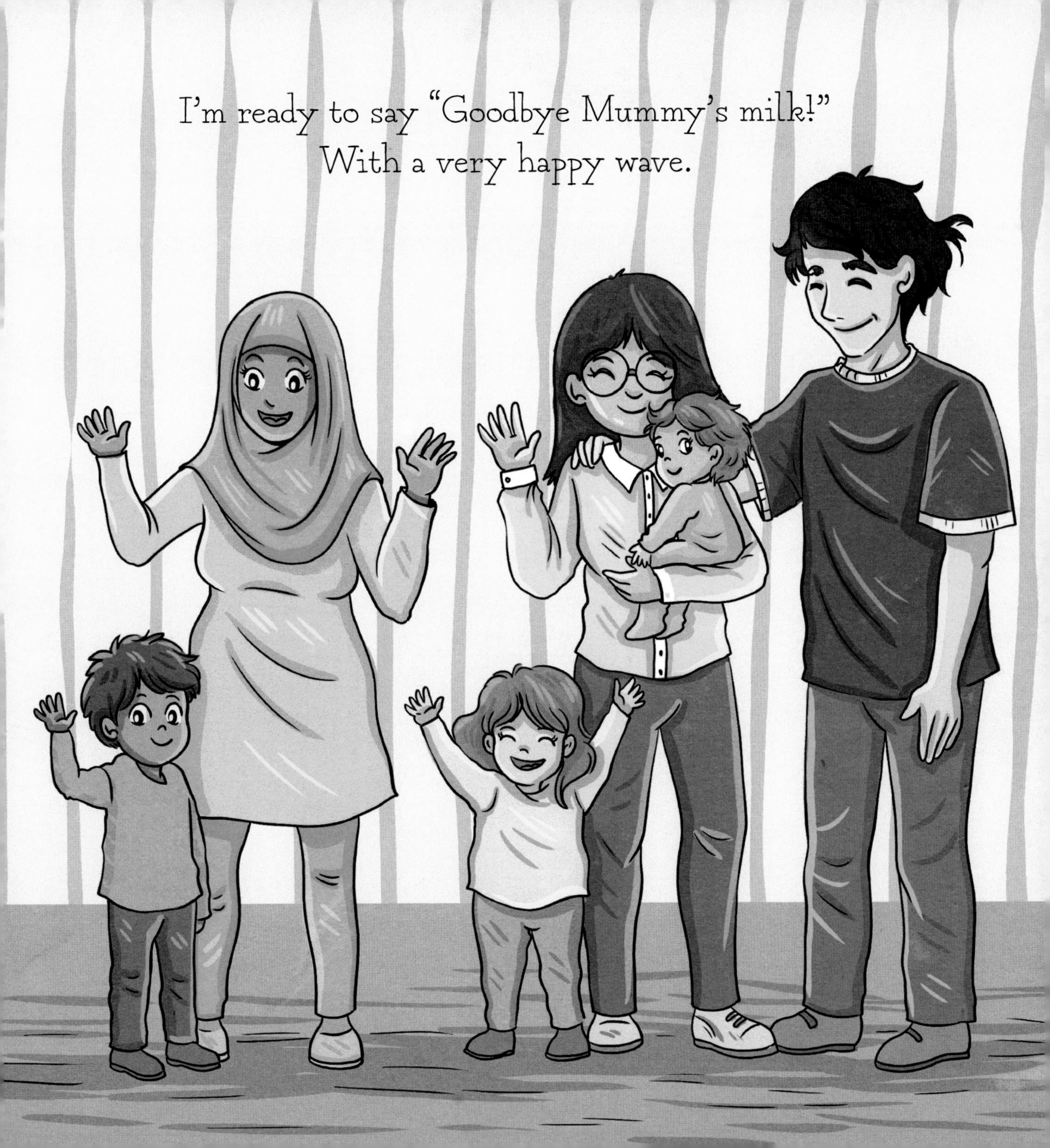
I'm ready to say "Goodbye Mummy's milk!"
With a very happy wave.

Record your breast/chestfeeding journey

I have breast/chestfed for ____________ days.

My Mummy's milk tastes like

____

The best thing about Mummy's milk is

____

My Mummy's milk makes me feel

____

My Mummy's milk has helped me

____

My favourite breast/chestfeeding memory

____

This is a picture of me drinking Mummy's milk.

By ______________________ Age ________

When I'm not drinking Mummy's milk I can...

Build a tower

Bake a cake

Ride a bike

Have a cuddle

Sleep together

Splash in puddles

Climb a tree

Build a den

Have a tea party

Go for a walk

Read a book

Paint a picture

Have a drink

Make up a story

Here are a few more ideas...

- Go camping
- Build sandcastles
- Go on an adventure
- Go to the park
- Go to the forest
- Go to playgroup
- Plant some flowers
- Collect insects in the garden
- Cook a meal
- Write a shopping list
- Play with my favourite toys
- Have a snack

Did this book help you or your little one in some way? Did you enjoy it? If so, please consider adding a review to the Goodbye Mummy's Milk! listing on Amazon.com. This will help the book reach more families. If you've finished with it - please share it, pass it on or donate it to your local infant feeding support group.

If you'd like to contact me, you can find me on Instagram @mariapaolaweeks.

Made in the USA
Las Vegas, NV
17 February 2024